EARLY THEMES

Ocean Life

WHALES, FISH, AND OTHER SEA CREATURES

by Kathleen M. Hollenbeck

SCHOLASTIC
PROFESSIONAL BOOKS

NEW YORK • TORONTO • LONDON • AUCKLAND • SYDNEY
MEXICO CITY • NEW DELHI • HONG KONG • BUENOS AIRES

For Judy and Bill, who love the ocean.

Edited by Joan Novelli
Cover design by Kelli Thompson
Cover art by Jo Lynn Alcorn
Interior design by Solutions by Design, Inc.
Interior illustrations by James Graham Hale
Poster design by Kathy Massaro
Poster illustration by Jo Lynn Alcorn

ISBN 0-439-18838-5

Contents

About This Book 4

Launching the Theme 7
  Passport to the Sea 8
  Make a Sea Life Mural 8
  Song of the Sea 9
  Reproducible Activity Pages 10–11

Whales and Other Sea Mammals 12
  Whale Tails 13
  Mammal Maze 14
  Calling All Whales 14
  Mammals of the Sea Riddles 15
  Which One's the Biggest? 16
  Reproducible Activity Pages 18–20

Fish 21
  Build a Fish 22
  Colors and Camouflage 23
  The Food Chain 23
  Mammal or Fish? 24
  Reproducible Activity Pages 25–28

Reptiles and Birds 29
  Reptile Rocks 30
  Sea Turtle Race 31
  How Sea Birds Find Food 32
  Flock of Feathers 33
  Reproducible Activity Pages 34–36

Other Sea Creatures 37
  No Bones About It! 38
  Make Your Own Jellyfish 38
  Oyster Math 40
  Wind and Waves 41
  Reproducible Activity Pages 42–44

Ocean Life Celebration 45

"What Do You See in the Sea?" poster . . . . bound in center

About This Book

Children and adults alike are drawn to the presence and power of the sea. Crashing waves, changing tides, and the endless expanse of sparkling water evoke emotions of awe, wonder, and excitement in even the youngest of hearts. Like the waters they live in, animals of the sea attract attention as well. Personifying grace under pressure, sea animals swim, scuttle, fly, and leap in and out of the water, carrying on their lives amid the thundering crash of waves or in the silence of their homes beneath the sea.

This book is designed to help you delve into the saltwater world. As you teach your students about sea mammals, fish, reptiles, birds, and invertebrates (animals without backbones), you'll shed light on a vast and intriguing population. You'll build bridges from curiosity to knowledge, giving children a solid base of wisdom they can count on every time they set foot in an aquarium or carry on a discussion about life in the sea.

Through hands-on activities, games, and discussions, your students will learn to differentiate between mammals and reptiles, invertebrates and fish. They'll look beyond the surface and realize that ocean waters are teeming with life, and that each bit of life is one part of a food chain. They will learn about the need for gills and fins and the benefits salty waters offer to the creatures that live there. In short, your students will begin to understand the nature of life in the sea.

WHAT'S INSIDE

Here are some of the resources you'll find in the pages that follow.

◎ **Launching the Theme:** activities for introducing the unit, getting a sense of what children know, and building excitement for what they'll learn

◎ **Learning Center Suggestions:** ideas for setting up an ocean-themed learning center and keeping the activity here going strong

◎ **Hands-On Activities:** step-by-step directions for guiding students in activities that connect every corner of the curriculum, including math, science, language arts, music, art, drama, and social studies

◎ **Reproducible Activity Pages:** more than a dozen age-appropriate, interactive reproducibles, designed to deepen children's understanding and promote hands-on involvement

◎ **Literature Connections:** book suggestions with related lessons to enrich learning

◎ **Ocean Life Celebration:** suggestions for wrapping up the unit

◎ **"What Do You See in the Sea?"** a colorful, informative poster displaying sea life from top to bottom, with accompanying activities

WHY TEACH WITH THEMES?

Themes integrate core skills with discovery. They allow children to revisit a topic again and again, examining it from all angles and within various subject areas, strengthening skills across the curriculum while deepening understanding, encouraging retention, building excitement, and motivating learning. Themes offer structure and direction, a detailed game plan for your goals.

With thematic teaching, you and your students can focus on a topic and explore it in depth without sacrificing the skills you're required to teach. Excited and eager to learn, your students will participate in and long remember the lessons you teach.

GETTING READY

Consider the following suggestions to help you get the most from your thematic unit.

◎ **Materials:** Each lesson contains a list of materials required for completing the activity. Look over the lists well in advance to be sure you have or can get what you need prior to presenting the lesson. You may want to inform families of your theme, opening the door for contributions from home. Families who have recently been to the seashore or aquarium may want to send in items of interest to enhance the learning center; others may wish to send in craft items or picture books on the theme.

◎ **Grouping:** Many of the lessons invite children to work in pairs or small groups. Create these groups each time the need arises or arrange them at the start, keeping them intact for the duration of the unit. If you choose to create long-term groups, allow group members to create their own name and logo to promote a cooperative atmosphere.

◎ **Assessment:** Thematic units offer many opportunities to assess student comprehension and development. As children decorate a sea mural (see page 8), sort fish from mammals in a card game (see page 24), and distinguish prey from predator (see page 23), you will be able to gauge their understanding of the topic. Store concrete proof of learning in manila folders, decorated by students and labeled with their names (and group logos, if applicable). Use folders to house theme-related artwork not on display, completed stories and reproducibles, and other projects.

SETTING UP A LEARNING CENTER

Few centers will be more pleasing to look at than one built around ocean life. Intricate and colorful, sea animals and scenery offer comfort and intrigue. Regardless of the theme, though, a good learning center requires a few basic ingredients to make it work well. A small table, several chairs, a bookshelf, and wall space form the foundation of a successful learning station. In addition, consider the following tips.

◎ **Decorate the Center:** Rugs, pillows, beanbag chairs, and stuffed animals go a long way toward making a learning center the place where children want to be. Tailor yours to reflect the sea theme, by adding stuffed seal pups, a makeshift lobster trap (black netting over a wooden crate turned on its side), and plenty of assorted reading materials. For visual appeal, display the "What Do You See in the Sea?" poster, magazine photos of sea animals, and any projects your students create during the unit.

◎ **Make It Their Center:** Be sure children view the learning center as their place to go to learn more about sea creatures, share what they've learned, and display their knowledge. Encourage them to share free time there, playing sea creature card games, participating in the Learning Center activities suggested throughout this book, and immersing themselves in sea life.

RESOURCES

Books

Amazing Fish by Mary Ling (Knopf, 1991). A myriad of fish swim across the pages of this mini-encyclopedia for young readers, providing a close look at fins, gills, camouflage, and many other aspects of life under the sea.

Extremely Weird Sea Creatures by Sarah Lovett (John Muir Publications, 1992). Dozens of interesting and amazing details fill the pages of this colorful, pictorial scrapbook of undersea life.

Let's Investigate: Slippery, Splendid Sea Creatures by Madelyn Wood Carlisle (Barron's Educational Series, 1993). This resource provides factual, easy-to-understand information about common sea animals such as dolphins, starfish, and crabs.

Sea Searcher's Handbook: Activities from the Monterey Bay Aquarium (Roberts Rinehart Publishers, 1996). Activities abound in this field guide for exploring

various seaside habitats, from rocky shore to deep sea. Although many of the activities are quite involved for young children, many can be adapted and used in some form, and the insight provided with them is authentic and invaluable.

Under the Sea from A to Z by Anne Doubilet (Crown, 1991). Take young readers on an alphabet walk underwater as they explore sea animals from anemones to zebra fish. Text is difficult for primary readers, but children will enjoy looking at the breathtaking photographs and associating each with a letter of the alphabet.

Web Sites

Check these Web sites to access colorful images, information, and additional resources on sea creatures:

www.mbayaq.org

www.oceanlight.com

www.seasky.org

Launching the Theme

Prepare your class for a journey through the sea—from sandy shore to deepest cavern. Create "passports" to record observations of animal life. Discover the buoyancy of salt water, and create a classroom mural your students can add to as they gain nautical knowledge.

SCIENCE NOTES

How wet is our world? Approximately two thirds of the Earth's surface is covered with water. Of this, only three percent is fresh water, suitable for drinking. The rest is salty and makes up the areas we know as the oceans or seas. Technically, large areas of water, such as the Atlantic Ocean, are called *oceans*. Smaller areas, such as the Caribbean, are called *seas*. In this book, the terms *ocean* and *sea* will be used interchangeably to indicate animals that live in salt water, regardless of the water's depth or size.

Passport to the Sea

Children make a passport to mark their journey through the world of whales and other sea creatures.

Materials

- ◎ Passport to the Sea reproducible (page 10)
- ◎ crayons
- ◎ scissors
- ◎ craft items, such as glue, yarn, colored sand, movable eyes, and pipe cleaners

Teaching the Lesson

1. Distribute a passport form to each child. Show children how to fold the passport along the dashed lines to make a book. Have children add construction-paper covers cut to size, then write their name and the title "Passport to the Sea" on the cover.

2. Invite children to trace the word on each page and talk about the animals they see. Have them name the ones they recognize.

3. As they learn about each new group of sea animals, have children color in and label the corresponding creatures. Children can use craft supplies to embellish their books, using pipe cleaners to make 3-D eels or giving sharks movable eyes.

Literature Connection

Bring a playful air to your classroom study of the sea with Douglas Florian's *In the Swim: Poems and Paintings* (Harcourt Brace, 1997). Florian's poems and the watercolors that accompany them are delightful and sometimes silly and are based on real water creatures such as the trout and manatee. Read aloud a poem a day and encourage children to imitate the author with their own cheery sea life poems and drawings.

Make a Sea Life Mural

Children will enjoy working together to create a backdrop for a mural that they will add to throughout the unit.

Materials

- ◎ white craft paper
- ◎ household sponges, cut into 2-inch squares
- ◎ blue tempera paint
- ◎ oversized shirts or smocks

Teaching the Lesson

1. Display a long strip of white craft paper on a bulletin board or wall.

2. Fill a small bowl with 2-inch sponge squares and another with several inches of blue tempera paint. Place these near the craft paper.

3. Have children wear oversized shirts or smocks to protect clothing. Let them dip the sponges in the paint, scrape off the excess, and press them against the white paper. They should continue sponge-painting until the entire surface of paper is covered, making a mottled seascape backdrop.

4 As they progress through the units, invite children to add to the mural with drawings and cutouts of sea animals and scenery.

Literature Connection Help children visualize the animals they'll add to their mural by traveling through Kate Needham's *The Great Undersea Search* (E D C Publications, 1996). As children set out to find the hidden sea animals, they'll learn oceans of information about undersea life. Other illustrated resources for young readers include two titles from Donald M. Silver's *One Small Square* series: *Coral Reef* (McGraw-Hill, 1997) and *Seashore* (McGraw-Hill, 1993).

Learning Center Link

Invite children to bring in books, magazines, stuffed animals, and pictures of sea animals. Arrange their contributions in the Learning Center. Place magazines and books in colorful milk crates or office organizers, neatly arranged and labeled for easy access.

SCIENCE NOTES

Why is seawater salty? Fresh water travels from streams and rivers to the sea. On its way, it runs over rocks and soil, picking up salts and other minerals, which it deposits in the sea. Other factors, such as evaporation (which takes fresh water from the sea and leaves the salt behind) and rainfall (which adds fresh water), also affect the amount of salt in the sea.

Song of the Sea

As you complete each section of the unit, teach the corresponding verse of the theme song "Song of the Sea" (see page 11)—and practice the previous verses if applicable. When you wrap up your unit with an Ocean Life Celebration (see page 45), children will be able to sing the whole song!

TIP: Make copies of the song for children to share with their families, too.

Literature Connection **Animals of the Sea**
Explore *Alphabet Sea* by Carolyn Spencer (Tortuga Books, 1999) and *Amazing Sea Creatures* by Andrew Brown (Crabtree, 1997) to learn more about sea animals named in the song. Help children locate the animals and learn what they look like. Let children sketch the various sea animals on paper plates and glue these to large tongue depressors. Sing the song again. Each time an animal's name is mentioned, have the child who holds its picture raise it for all to see.

Literature Connection Take a trip underwater with Joanna Cole's *The Magic School Bus on the Ocean Floor* (Scholastic, 1992). Follow Ms. Frizzle from seashore to coral reef as she gives her students a firsthand, comprehensive view of life in and around the sea. After reading, invite children to draw a picture illustrating one fact they've learned from the book.

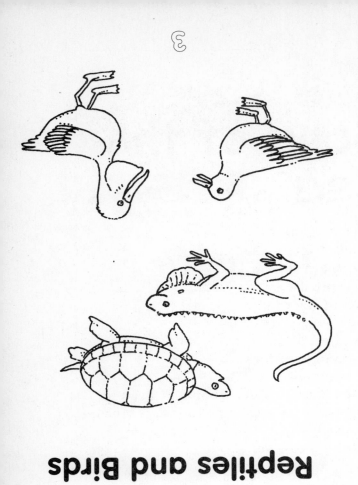

3

Reptiles and Birds

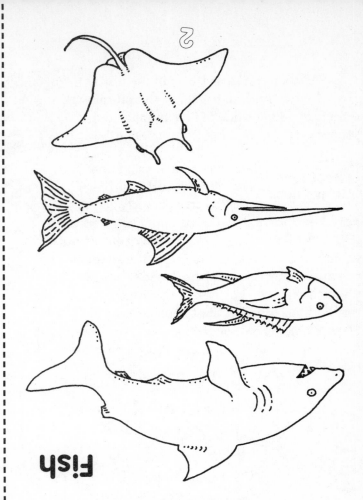

2

Fish

Invertebrates

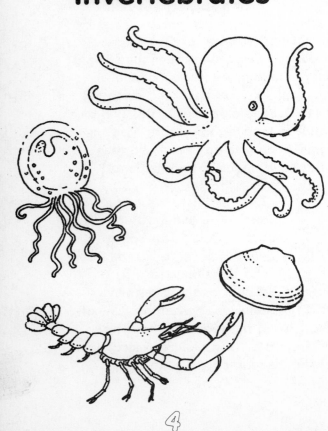

4

Mammals

1

Song of the Sea

(sing to the tune of "B-I-N-G-O")

A mammal is an animal
That drinks milk from its mother.
Whale and porpoise, too,
Walrus, dolphin, seal,
All have blood that's warm
And every one's a mammal.

A fish needs gills to help it breathe
And fins to help it swim.
Shark and manta ray,
Haddock, tuna fish,
Grouper, moray eel,
Yes, every one's a fish.

Birds and reptiles live on land
And also in the water.
Lizards, turtles do.
Reptiles are these two.
Sea gulls, pelicans
Are birds that live near water.

Invertebrates are soft inside
Because they have no backbone.
Starfish, octopus,
Lobster, crab, and clam,
They crawl, float, and swim.
Invertebrates they all are.

Early Themes: Ocean Life Scholastic Professional Books

Whales and Other Sea Mammals

When children think of sea animals, familiar images of whales, dolphins, and seals spring to mind. Sporting long, torpedo-shaped bodies flanked with flippers and fins, these animals represent the freedom and strength of life in the deep, open sea. They also share one more characteristic: They are mammals. Warm-blooded, nurturing creatures, sea mammals are part of a small but mighty crew. In this section, you'll find activities for exploring the ways they move, the foods they eat, and their unique modes of communication.

SCIENCE NOTES

Mammals do not lay eggs. Instead, they give birth to live young. Some sea mammals (such as whales) give birth in water. Others (such as seals) give birth on land.

Whale Tails

Children decorate whale tails and learn that scientists identify whales by the unique markings on their tails.

Materials

◎ Whale Tails reproducible (see page 18)
◎ black crayons or markers

Teaching the Lesson

1. Explain that scientists can tell whales apart from one another. Humpback whales have markings or patterns on the underside of their flukes—the two flat halves that make up the tail. Each humpback whale has its own unique markings. By looking at the flukes, scientists can identify specific whales and track their migration.

2. Give each child two copies of the reproducible. Have children use black crayon to draw markings on one of their tails. Their markings should be bold and easy to see, such as stripes or spots.

3. Divide the class in half. Assign one half the job of "whale" and the other, "scientist." Have the whales sit facing the scientists. Ask each scientist to have a black crayon and the blank reproducible ready.

4. At your command, have all whales hold up their tails for 20 seconds while each scientist chooses one whale tail and studies it closely. When the time is up, whales must "dive" (hide their tails). On the blank reproducible, scientists should draw details they remember about the tail they studied.

5. Ask whales to wave their tails again. How accurate are the scientists' drawings? Let scientists and whales reverse roles and try the activity again.

Literature Connection
Embark on a hilarious sea adventure with Chris Van Dusen's *Down to the Sea with Mr. Magee* (Chronicle Books, 2000). When Mr. Magee takes a trip to the sea, he gets more than he bargained for, thanks to the antics of a playful whale. Let children take turns acting out the roles of the whale, Mr. Magee, and his dog. Use a large cardboard box for a boat that Mr. Magee and his dog can fit snugly inside—and get out of in a hurry!

ACTIVITY Extension
Fish have vertical tails that move from side to side. Whales do not. Instead, whales have flat back-fins called *flukes*. Whales beat their flukes up and down to push themselves through the water. They also use flippers to help them dive and steer. Let children say the words *flukes* and *flippers* aloud several times. What do they notice? Play a game to reinforce this spelling pattern (*fl*). Cut out a picture of a whale, complete with flukes and flippers. Gather children in a circle and start the game by saying a word that starts with the letters *fl*. Pass the whale to another child, who says a new word that starts with *fl*. Continue, until everyone has had a turn or you run out of *fl* words. Children who wish to can pass on their turns and simply hand the whale to someone else.

Mammal Maze

Children move through a maze, answering questions about the properties of a mammal.

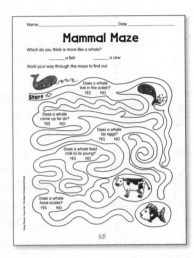

Materials

◎ Mammal Maze reproducible (see page 19)

◎ pencils

Teaching the Lesson

1 Give each child a copy of the activity page. Help children identify the animals at the top of the page.

2 Have children proceed through the maze from start to finish. Encourage children not to shout out answers so everyone will have the opportunity to consider each question.

Literature Connection Take a trip to Alaska, where a walrus calf accompanies its mother to its summer feeding grounds in *Little Walrus Warning* by Carol Young (Soundprints, 1996). Invite children to compare the walrus's connection with its mother to their own relationship with a caregiver. How old will the walrus be when it is considered an adult? How old will children be when they are considered adults? Discuss the migratory needs of the walrus and other sea animals, such as the seal. Why do the animals travel to different regions as the seasons change?

Learning Center Link

Children will enjoy making their own mazes to share with classmates. Review the basic structure and goal of a maze. Invite children to make new mazes that incorporate what they've learned. Photocopy the mazes and place them at the Learning Center for all to enjoy.

Calling All Whales

Children shake noisemakers to illustrate aspects of animal communication in the sea.

Materials

◎ empty film canisters with lids

◎ marbles, popcorn kernels, uncooked rice, jingle bells, beans

Teaching the Lesson

1 Make mini-noisemakers by filling the canisters with marbles, popcorn kernels, uncooked rice, jingle bells, or beans. Secure lids. Be sure to make at least two of each kind of noisemaker.

2 Explain that whales and dolphins talk to each other by making special sounds such as squeals, clicks, and whistles. They use sounds to communicate and to *echolocate* (find prey and navigate by bouncing sounds off animals, objects, and the environment). Tell children that today they will communicate as if they are whales.

3 Hand out the canisters at random. Let children walk around the room, shaking their canisters and listening carefully to find those that make the same sound as their own.

Literature Connection Find out what the saying "as big as a whale" really means! Share Nicola Davies' *Big Blue Whale* (Candlewick Press, 1997). In words and pictures, the author and illustrator describe how it feels to touch a whale and compare the whale's size to that of other large animals, such as an elephant. After reading the story, provide wet soap and a real hard-boiled egg—sans the shell. Let children close their eyes and pretend they are touching a whale. While you're at it, you might simulate other sea animal sensations as well, such as sandpaper for a shark.

ACTIVITY Extension How does a whale make sound? One way is by squeezing pockets of air near its blowhole. Let children test this process with balloons. Have each child inflate a balloon and then stretch the neck to let the air out. The air will make a shrill, squealing sound as it is released. In the same way, whales initiate vibrations as they squeeze the pouches of air. These vibrations produce sounds that can be heard miles away.

Learning Center Link

Place a new set of film-canister noisemakers at the Learning Center, along with index cards on which you've written the name of what's inside each canister and glued a sample of it. Write a number on the back of each index card and on the corresponding canister. Let children shake the canisters, then match them to the index cards. They can turn over the cards to self-check their work.

Mammals of the Sea Riddles

Children solve riddles to identify sea mammals.

Materials

◎ reference materials on seals, dolphins, and other sea mammals

Teaching the Lesson

1 Invite children to recall what makes an animal a mammal: *It breathes air, has warm blood, gives birth to live young, and nurses its young.* Explain that other mammals live in the sea as well: the seal, dolphin, walrus, and sea otter.

2 Each day as students explore sea mammals, post a riddle that provides clues about a sea mammal without naming it. (See samples, below.)

I am a very small whale.
I have fins and a wide, flat tail.
I come to the surface to breathe.
I am a fast, graceful swimmer.
What am I? (*dolphin*)

I am the largest of all animals.
I have baleen instead of teeth.
I eat plankton and tiny ocean creatures.
When I breathe, air shoots from my blowhole.
What am I? (*blue whale*)

I spend most of my time in water.
I pull myself onto land to rest or give birth.
My fur and a thick layer of fat keep me warm.
I can stay underwater for 30
    minutes before I need air.
What am I? (*seal*)

I am a huge, heavy animal.
My teeth can grow to be three feet long!
I find food on the ocean floor.
Thick layers of fat keep
   my body warm.
What am I? (*walrus*)

I have whiskers and fur.
I have a long tail and webbed feet.
I wrap myself in seaweed at night while I sleep.
This keeps me from floating out to sea.
What am I? (*sea otter*)

3 Cut a slit in the top of a covered shoebox and invite children to write their answers to each riddle on a sheet of paper and place it inside. Encourage research skills by having children include sources with their answers.

4 At the end of the day, reveal the answer. Invite children to share some of the sources they used to solve the riddle.

Literature Connection Bring a sea otter close to children's hearts with *Lootas Little Wave Eater: An Orphaned Sea Otter's Story* by Clare Hodgson Meeker (Sasquatch Books, 1999). Have children fold paper into four sections and draw four pictures that highlight the important details in Lootas' life: her adoption by the Seattle Aquarium, her contact with humans, her introduction to other otters, and finally, her release into the sea. For free-time reading, introduce *Seals, Sea Lions, and Walruses* by Judith Walker-Hodge (Barrons Juveniles, 1999). Children will enjoy the dramatic photographs of these well-loved mammals in their natural habitats.

Learning Center Link

Post a sheet of chart paper at the center for each of several sea mammals. Label the chart paper with each animal's name. Invite children to use the resources at the center to find information about each animal. Have them add facts and pictures with captions to the charts to create a collaborative presentation about each animal.

MATH

Which One's the Biggest?

Children sort baleen whales and toothed whales, then graph them by size.

Materials

◎ Which One's the Biggest? reproducible (see page 20)

◎ markers or crayons

◎ scissors

◎ chart paper

◎ glue stick

Teaching the Lesson

1 Explain that there are two different kinds of whales: *toothed whales* (whales with teeth) and *baleen whales* (whales with baleen instead of teeth). Toothed whales grasp animals or plants with their teeth, tearing and chewing. Baleen whales fill their mouths with water and then push it back out through comb-like filters called *baleen*. Baleen holds back tiny sea life for the whale to swallow.

2 Draw a graph on paper. Be sure the graph has ten columns (one for each whale) and that it is numbered along the left side to represent increments of ten feet. Use the largest and smallest whales on the reproducible as a guide. Glue a picture of each whale at the bottom of each column.

3 Give each child a reproducible page. Identify the whales together. Ask children to cut out the whales and sort them into two groups: *baleen* (Right whale, Bowhead whale, Gray whale, Blue whale, Humpback whale) and *toothed* (Sperm whale, Beaked whale, Beluga whale, porpoise, Pilot whale).

4 Invite volunteers to come up and color in the bars on the graph one at a time to show how big the whales are.

5 Examine the graph with questions, such as *Which whale is largest? Which is smallest? How much bigger is a [ ] than a [ ] whale? Which group of whales seems to have larger animals—baleen or toothed?*

6 Let children use their whale pictures to create their own graphs, using the class graph as a model.

Learning Center Link

Fill a dishpan with warm water and one cup of rice. Stir the water so the rice is evenly distributed. Let children dip a small food strainer into the water and scoop up some rice and water. As children lift the strainer, water will drain out and rice will remain behind. Liken this to the baleen whale, which strains seawater to catch tiny sea life for food.

ACTIVITY Extension Provide string cut to match the length of various whales—for example, porpoise (5 feet) and Sowerby's whale (13 feet). Tape a label on each so that children know which whale the string represents. Let children use the string as a nonstandard unit of measure to find things that are about the same size as the whales. Encourage children to be creative. For example, they might find that four classmates lined up head to toe on the floor are as long as a Sowerby's whale. Have children record their findings on chart paper labeled "As Big as a [whale's name]."

Literature Connection Find the answers to dozens of questions about whales in *Do Whales Have Belly Buttons? Questions and Answers About Whales and Dolphins* by Melvin and Gilda Berger (Scholastic, 1999). Use the book's question-and-answer format to reinforce early research skills. Let children choose one question from the book, read its answer, and create a cartoon to illustrate the concept they have learned.

TIP: Wrap up this section of your theme unit by singing the first verse of the theme song.

Song of the Sea
(to the tune of "B-I-N-G-O")

A mammal is an animal
That drinks milk from its mother.
Whale and porpoise, too,
Walrus, dolphin, seal,
All have blood that's warm
And every one's a mammal.

Whale Tails

Early Themes: Ocean Life Scholastic Professional Books

Mammal Maze

Which do you think is more like a whale?

_____ a fish   _____ a cow

Work your way through the maze to find out.

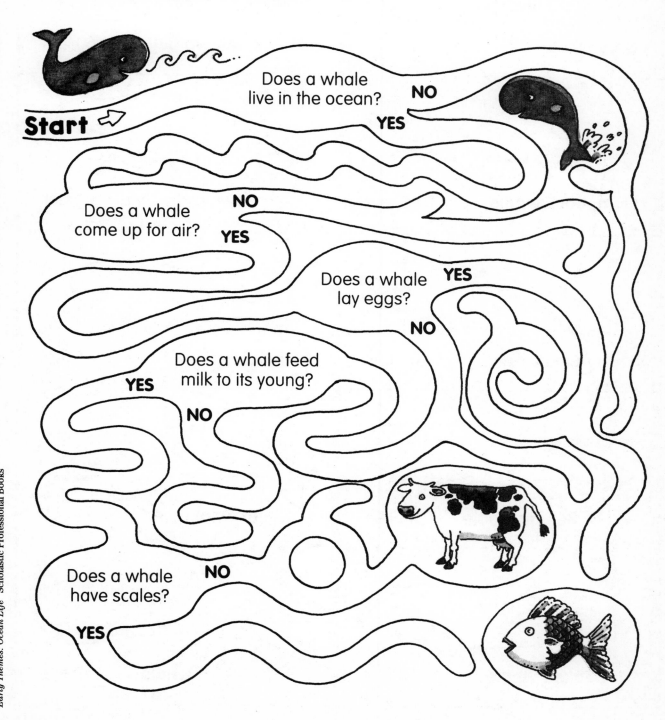

Start ⇨

Does a whale live in the ocean?   **NO**   **YES**

Does a whale come up for air?   **NO**   **YES**

Does a whale lay eggs?   **YES**   **NO**

Does a whale feed milk to its young?   **YES**   **NO**

Does a whale have scales?   **NO**   **YES**

Name_____ Date_____

Which One's the Biggest?

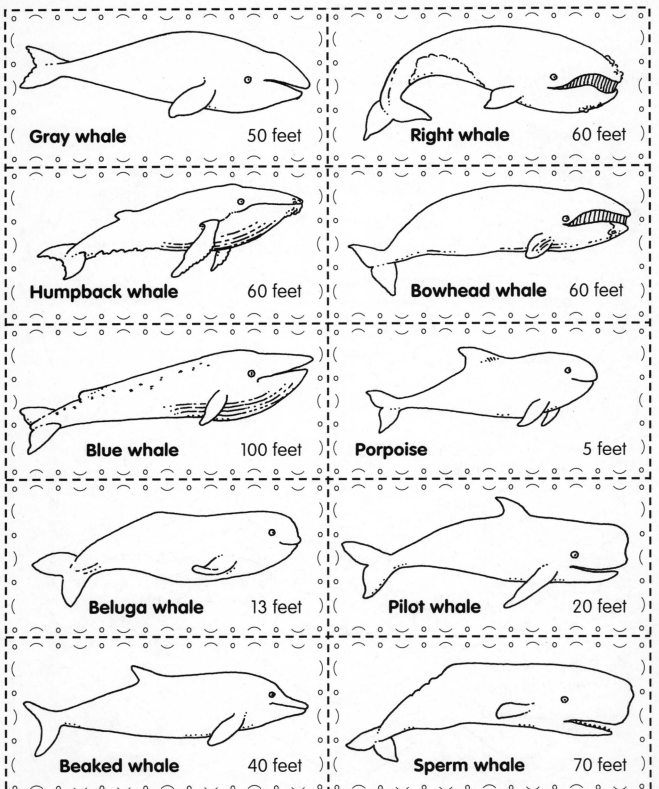

Gray whale   50 feet

Right whale   60 feet

Humpback whale   60 feet

Bowhead whale   60 feet

Blue whale   100 feet

Porpoise   5 feet

Beluga whale   13 feet

Pilot whale   20 feet

Beaked whale   40 feet

Sperm whale   70 feet

Early Themes: Ocean Life Scholastic Professional Books

Fish

From the tiniest goby to the largest whale shark, fish embody the essence of life in the sea. Free-swimming, fast-moving, water-dependent creatures, fish dwell in shallow tide pools and deep canyons. Both prey and predator, they come in all shapes, colors, and sizes. The activities in this section explore fish and their ways of life—how they move and breathe, what they eat, and how they defend and protect themselves.

SCIENCE NOTES

Small fish eat tiny sea animals and plants. They in turn are often eaten by larger fish, who are eaten by still larger fish, and so on. To protect themselves, fish rely on various means of defense and protection, including camouflage (by which body shapes, patterns, and colors help fish blend with surroundings); body shape (which allows fish to hide or escape; fish shaped like snakes can hide within crevices or wriggle under sand; others are shaped like torpedos for speed); venom (which allows a fish to inject enemies with poison); sharp, spiked, or spiny bodies (which prevent predators from biting); and swimming in schools (which can confuse predators and shield individual fish from attack).

Build a Fish

Children construct a fish and learn the purpose of its gills, fins, and scales.

Materials

◎ Build a Fish reproducible (see page 25)
◎ scissors
◎ glue sticks
◎ crayons or markers
◎ string

Teaching the Lesson

1 Give each child a copy of the reproducible. Help children read the name of each body part and its description.

2 Allow time for children to cut out, assemble, and color their fish.

3 Attach string to each fish and hang from the ceiling. Then play a guessing game. Invite children to solve the following riddles:

I am a coat of armor for a fish.
I protect fish from germs.
I make it easier to glide through the water.
What am I? (*scales*)

We help fish move and steer.
We help fish keep their balance.
Without us, a fish might sink.
What are we? (*fins*)

You will find us on the sides of a fish.
We help fish get oxygen from water.
Without us, a fish could not breathe.
What are we? (*gills*)

Learning Center Link

Let children take a closer look at one fish—the shark—with this bookmaking activity. Provide copies of the shark pattern on page 26. Have children cut out the pattern and trace it to make pages for a book. Have them put the pages together and staple them at one end. Let children use books and other reference materials to learn more about sharks, then record facts in their shark-shaped books. Some facts to start with follow.

◎ *Sharks have several rows of teeth. Every two weeks, a new, razor-sharp row moves forward to replace the old front row.*

◎ *The whale shark is the world's biggest fish. It can grow to be almost 60 feet long!*

◎ *Shark jaws are strong. Large sharks can bend steel bars with their jaws!*

Literature Connection Read aloud Leo Lionni's *Swimmy* (Pantheon, 1963), the charming tale of a fish who teaches his peers a creative method of swimming in schools. Follow up by letting children experiment with the artist's techniques. Cut fish shapes out of sponges. Let children dip the shapes in paint and press them on paper again and again to create their own uniquely shaped schools. Reinforce math skills: Ask children to estimate the number of fish they see in a classmate's artwork, then count them.

Colors and Camouflage

Children use craft supplies to decorate fish and blend them with their natural environment.

Materials

- unlined paper
- scissors
- glue stick
- construction paper
- tissue paper, pipe cleaners in various colors, colored sand, crayons, markers

Teaching the Lesson

1. Explain that some fish protect themselves from enemies with camouflage. Their bodies look the same as the seaweed, water, or sand around them. Ask children to guess why a fish might have a body that matches its environment. (*So that its* predators—*the animals that hunt it for food—will have a harder time seeing and catching it.*)

2. Draw the outline of a fish on a sheet of unlined paper. Photocopy one for each child in your class. Ask each child to cut out the fish and glue it to a sheet of construction paper (positioned horizontally).

3. Invite children to draw an ocean scene around the fish, making seaweed out of tissue paper or pipe cleaners, sprinkling colored sand over glue for a sea-bottom effect, and adding water and sea life with crayons or markers. Ask children to color their fish to match the background scenes they have drawn, in effect camouflaging by pattern and/or color.

The Food Chain

Children join hands to make a food chain.

Materials

- index cards (or name tags)

Teaching the Lesson

1. Invite children to review a basic food chain from life on land. (See sample, above.) Draw it on the chalkboard or on chart paper as a simple flow chart. Explain that just as there are food chains on land, there are also food chains in the ocean.

2. Assign each child the role of a plant, fish, or mammal of the sea. Write the child's role on an index card (or name tag). Remember to include the following: plankton (tiny plant life), small fish (anchovy, goby), medium fish (haddock, mackerel), large fish (tuna, shark), and sea mammal (dolphin, whale). You'll also want to have one child start the food chain by playing the part of the sun.

3. Have the "sun" come to the front of the room and invite "plankton" to join him or her and hold hands to form a chain.

4. Invite "animals that eat plankton" to step forward and join the chain. These will include small and medium fish.

5 Continue in this manner, with larger fish following smaller fish. There will be exceptions to the chain, such as baleen whales, which eat plankton rather than fish.

Literature Connection Find fodder for graphs and group projects in *The Amazing Book of Fish Records and Other Ocean Creatures: The Largest, the Smallest, the Fastest, and Many More* by Samuel G. Woods (Blackbirch Marketing, 2000). With children's help, make a classroom calendar (with or without lift-up flaps), revealing one amazing fish or sea creature fact for each day of the month.

MATH/CRITICAL THINKING

Mammal or Fish?

Children sort creature cards to categorize mammals and fish.

Materials
- Mammal or Fish? reproducible (see pages 27 and 28)
- scissors

Teaching the Lesson

1 Help children recall differences between mammals and fish—for example, mammals breathe air, drink milk, and are warm-blooded. Fish breathe underwater, have gills and scales (in most cases), and are cold-blooded.

2 Hand out the reproducible (using the two blank cards to add creatures of your choice), and help children identify the sea creatures pictured. Have children cut out the cards along the dotted lines.

3 Let children work independently or in small groups to sort the cards into groups based on whether each creature is a fish or a mammal. Provide resources students can use independently if they need help deciding which group an animal belongs in.

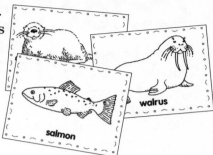

walrus

salmon

ACTIVITY Extension For an added challenge, have each child pick five cards at random and write a number sentence based on the number of mammals and fish they have picked—for example, 3 mammals + 2 fish = 5 sea animals. Continue this for several rounds of play, or let children pair off and use the cards to play common card games such as "Go Fish" and "Concentration."

Literature Connection Stretch the imagination and strengthen counting skills with Lois Ehlert's *Fish Eyes: A Book You Can Count On* (Harcourt Brace, 1992). Have children count with you as you read through the rhyming story. Then invite them to don imaginary fins and scales, and draw their own numerical trip under the sea. Have children draw fish, grouping them in various ways to reach the same sum (e.g., 4 fish + 4 fish = 8 fish; 5 fish + 3 fish = 8 fish, and so on).

TIP: Wrap up this section of your theme unit by singing verse two of the theme song. Practice the first one, too! (See page 11.)

Song of the Sea
(to the tune of "B-I-N-G-O")

A fish needs gills to help it breathe
And fins to help it swim.
Shark and manta ray,
Haddock, tuna fish,
Grouper, moray eel,
Yes, every one's a fish.

Build a Fish

 ### Gills

Gills are small slits on the sides of a fish.
Gills help fish breathe underwater.
Water has oxygen in it.
Fish need oxygen to live.
Gills help fish take oxygen from water.

gill

 ### Fins

Fins are like arms for a fish.
Fins help fish move through the water.
Fins help fish swim and steer.
They help fish float and dive.

fin

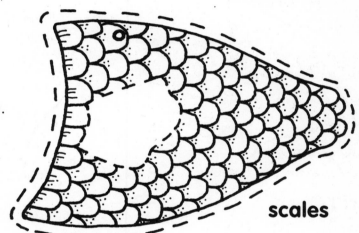

Scales

Scales cover the body of a fish.
Scales help protect the fish.
Scales are slippery.
They help fish move quickly.

scales

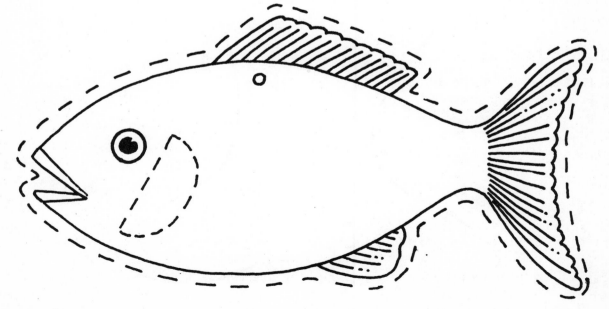

Make a Shark Shape Book

Early Themes: Ocean Life Scholastic Professional Books

Mammal or Fish?

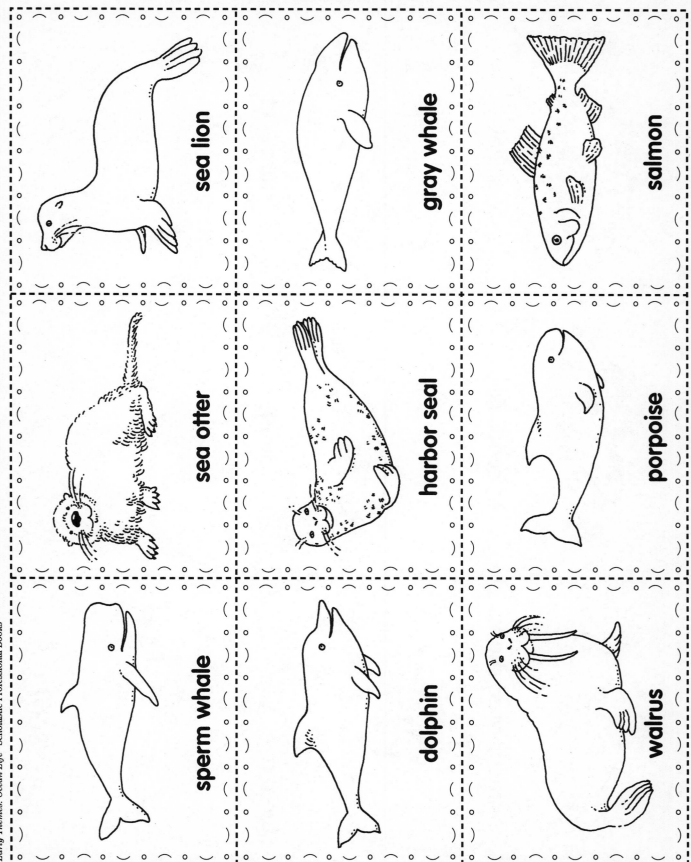

sea lion

gray whale

salmon

sea otter

harbor seal

porpoise

sperm whale

dolphin

walrus

Early Themes: Ocean Life Scholastic Professional Books

Mammal or Fish?

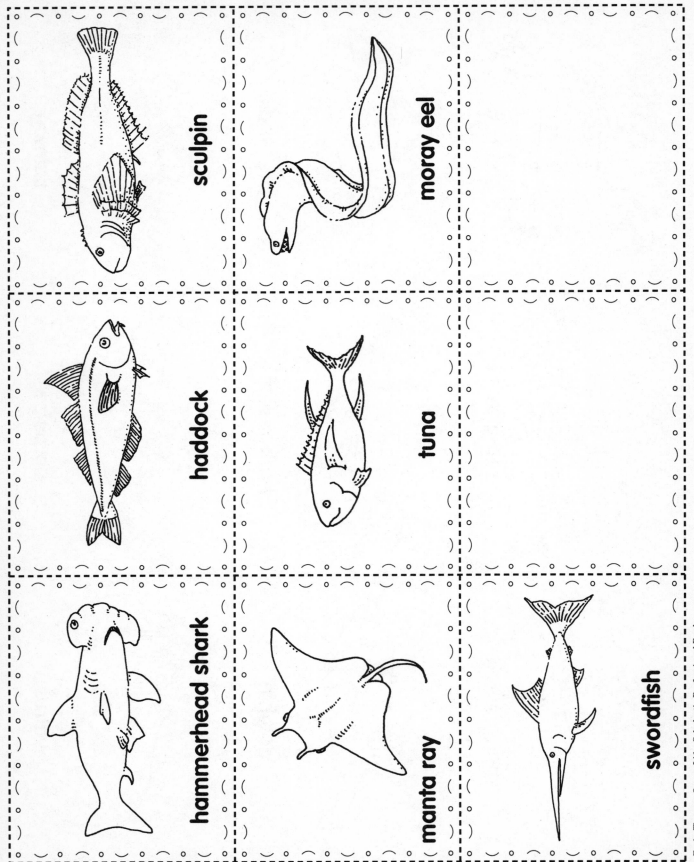

sculpin

moray eel

haddock

tuna

hammerhead shark

manta ray

swordfish

Early Themes: Ocean Life Scholastic Professional Books

Reptiles and Birds

Marine reptiles and birds live in and near the ocean, yet in much smaller numbers than on land. In this section, students examine characteristics of marine reptiles and birds, learning who they are, where and how they live, and how they adapt to their environment.

SCIENCE NOTES

Few reptiles live in the ocean. The marine iguana is the only lizard living in the sea. Like the turtle, it swims, eats sea plants, and comes to the surface for air. There are more than 50 species of sea snakes. Most live in tropical waters. Some hatch eggs inside their bodies and release them at sea. The saltwater crocodile is the world's largest reptile. It lives in eastern regions such as India and Asia and can swim in the open sea. The body of a sea bird is well adapted to life in a harsh, demanding climate. (See page 32 for more information.)

Reptile Rocks

Children test the effects of air and water temperature on rocks to understand the cold-blooded nature of reptiles.

Materials

- ◎ My Reptile Log reproducible (see page 34)
- ◎ small rocks (2–3 inches in diameter)
- ◎ plastic containers (12–16 ounce size)
- ◎ water
- ◎ table lamp with bendable neck
- ◎ ice cubes

Teaching the Lesson

1. Set up the stations listed on the Reptile Log, providing a heat source (lamp), and bowls of cold, warm, and hot water.

2. Remind children that humans are mammals: They are warm-blooded. Even in cold temperatures, mammals can stay warm as long as they have enough clothing, fur, or fat to hold in the warmth of their blood. Explain that reptiles and birds are not mammals. Their body temperature changes to match the air, water, and land around them.

3. Give each child one rock and a Reptile Log. Ask children to pretend the rocks are reptiles. Have them record predictions on the Reptile Log, circling how they think their rocks will feel in each situation.

4. Divide the class into groups. Have groups move from station to station, remaining at each for 10–15 minutes. (Change the water at the stations as needed to keep it at the right temperature.) After completing each station, have children circle results. Bring them together to share and compile results.

ACTIVITY Extension Make reptile puzzles to reinforce counting and number recognition. Enlarge the reptile patterns. (See below.) Trace a reptile on tagboard. Using thick, black marker, draw a jagged line to divide the reptile pattern in half. On one side of the line, write a number. On the other side of the line, draw a group of dots to represent that number. Laminate the puzzle, then cut it in half on the jagged line. Repeat to make one for each student (each with a different number). Place one half of a puzzle on each child's desk. Mix up the other halves and give one to each child. Have children circulate around the room, looking for the other half of their puzzle. When a child finds it, have him or her put the puzzle together and sit down in that seat. When everyone has made a puzzle, mix up the pieces and play again.

Learning Center Link

Gather assorted rubber or plastic "reptiles" to display at the center. (Children might like to bring in some of their own to share.) Each day, post a different activity for children to try. Suggestions follow.

◎ *Sort the reptiles into two groups and record the sorting rule.*

◎ *Use reference materials to find the name of each reptile. Arrange the reptiles in alphabetical order.*

◎ *Write a mini-play with a partner. Let the reptiles play the starring roles. Change your voice to play the part of each reptile.*

MATH

Sea Turtle Race

Children solve math problems in a race with walnut-shell turtles.

Materials

◎ masking tape

◎ empty walnut shell halves

◎ felt, movable eyes

◎ markers

◎ scissors

◎ glue

◎ dice

Teaching the Lesson

1. Place strips of masking tape at 4-inch intervals along the length of a long table.

2. Give each child one walnut shell half, scraps of felt, and movable eyes or markers. Have children decorate the shell as a sea turtle, gluing on a felt head and flippers and adding eyes. They might also add shell patterns with marker.

3. Divide the class into groups of four or six. Allow each group to race their turtles at the table marked with tape. To run the race, children roll one die, count the dots on top, and move their turtle forward that number of lines. The first turtle to reach the last line is the winner.

ACTIVITY Extension Divide the class into groups of three or four each. Give each group a sheet of posterboard. Have children work together to create Sea Turtle Race game boards. Encourage children to illustrate the game boards, using what they know about a sea turtle's habitat for ideas. Let children explain how to play their games, then set them up at a Learning Center for classmates to play.

Literature Connection Share Helen Ward's *The Hare and the Tortoise: A Fable from Aesop* (Millbrook Press, 1999) or Janet Stevens's *The Tortoise and the Hare* (Holiday House, 1984). Have children rewrite the story so the race takes place in or by the sea. Which sea animal will take the place of the hare? What kinds of scenery will the marine turtle and its opponent race past? Who will cheer them on? Which animal will win the race, and how?

How Sea Birds Find Food

Children make a lift-the-flap book that shows how marine birds catch their prey. To learn more about sea birds, see Science Notes, right.

Materials

◎ How Sea Birds Find Food reproducible (see page 35)

◎ scissors

◎ glue sticks

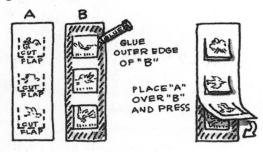

Teaching the Lesson

1 Give each child a copy of How Sea Birds Find Food. Have children cut out the book on the solid lines, then cut along the dashed line at the center to make two sections.

2 Guide children in following these steps to make their books:

◎ Cut along the dashed lines on section A to make three flaps.

◎ Apply glue along the four edges of section B.

◎ Place section A over section B and press to join the pages.

◎ Lift the flaps to learn where each kind of bird finds its food and what it eats.

SCIENCE NOTES

Feathers provide a thick, waterproof covering to protect birds from coldness and wetness. Webbed feet aid in swimming or perching on water. A broad wingspan allows sea birds to fly for hours at a time, crossing hundreds of miles a day in search of food. (Penguins don't fly, but use their wings to steer underwater.) Straight, sharp beaks suit birds that dive headfirst into the water. Hooked beaks help birds dig in sand and hold squirming prey. Wide beaks carry multiple fish at one time.

Literature Connection
Share Bobbie Kalman's *Marine Birds* (Crabtree, 1997), which offers a dazzling look at birds that live near the ocean. Penguins, pelicans, and albatross are among those featured on the pages of this colorful, informative book designed for young readers. Ask each child to choose a favorite bird from the book and write two facts about it on paper. Invite volunteers to read their facts aloud while others guess which mystery bird they like best.

ACTIVITY Extension
Use liquid eraser to make a blank copy of the lift-the-flap book on page 35. Provide children with copies of the template and reference material on sea birds. Let them work with partners to make new lift-the-flap books about what they learn.

Flock of Feathers

Children create number sentences with feathers and birds.

Materials

◎ Flock of Feathers reproducible (see page 36)

◎ scissors

◎ crayons

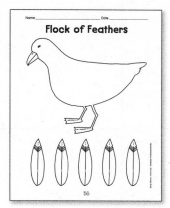

Teaching the Lesson

1 Divide the class into pairs. Give each pair two bird and ten feather patterns. Have children cut out and color the bird and feather patterns.

2 Let partners take turns placing feathers on each bird to make an addition equation—for example, four feathers on one bird and three on the other.

3 Ask each child to look at the way his/her partner has arranged the feathers. Ask: *How many feathers do you see on the first bird? How many feathers do you see on the second bird? How many feathers are there all together?*

4 Have children write the number sentences on a sheet of paper. Invite children to create other feather combinations, writing additional number sentences as they work together.

ACTIVITY Extension Draw the shape of a sea bird on cardboard and cut it out, leaving behind a sturdy stencil. Let children take turns using the stencil, painting inside the entire shape to create sea birds on a sheet of drawing paper. Encourage children to embellish their paintings with realistic seaside scenery, such as waves, rocky cliffs, seaweed, and fish.

Literature Connection Can your students guess how the Oystercatcher got its name? Learn more about this sea bird and others in *One Small Square: Seashore* by Donald M. Silver (Freeman, 1993). From what birds feed on to how gulls stay in the same spot while waves move forward, this book is full of intriguing information and detailed illustrations.

TIP: Wrap up this section of your theme unit by singing the third verse of the theme song. Practice the first two, as well! (See page 11.)

Song of the Sea
(to the tune of "B-I-N-G-O")

Birds and reptiles live on land
And also in the water.
Lizards, turtles do.
Reptiles are these two.
Sea gulls, pelicans
Are birds that live near water.

My Reptile Log

If my rock is...	I think it will feel...			I found out that it feels...		
Station 1 under a lamp	cold	warm	hot	cold	warm	hot
Station 2 in hot water	cold	warm	hot	cold	warm	hot
Station 3 in ice water	cold	warm	hot	cold	warm	hot
Station 4 in warm water	cold	warm	hot	cold	warm	hot

Early Themes: Ocean Life Scholastic Professional Books

How Sea Birds Find Food

A

Cormorant

Storm Petrel

Great Skua

B

The cormorant dives to find fish.

The petrel catches fish as it flies.

The skua steals fish from other birds.

Flock of Feathers

Other Sea Creatures

What do sand dollars, starfish, and clams have in common? They are *invertebrates*—creatures without backbones that float, jet, and swim through the sea. The activities in this section follow these extraordinary creatures over whitecaps and seabed, exploring the ways they move and eat, the unique characteristics of their bodies, and the undersea worlds they inhabit.

SCIENCE NOTES

Invertebrates move in a variety of ways. Some depend on currents, while others propel themselves. For example, the scallop flaps its shells together, forcing out jets of water that push it backward. The octopus uses arms to pull itself through the water. It also shoots jets of water out of its body to help it swim fast. The jellyfish floats on water, drifting with the current. The purple sea snail makes its own raft of bubbles. The bubbles float on the water, and the sea snail clings to them.

No Bones About It!

See-through pictures let children identify invertebrates at a glance.

Materials

◎ No Bones About It! reproducible (see pages 42–43)

◎ pencils

Teaching the Lesson

1. Invite children to recall the names of some fish, such as tuna, sculpin, eel, and swordfish. Explain that each of these animals has fins, gills, and a backbone.

2. Explain that not all animals in the sea have backbones. Animals without backbones are called *invertebrates*.

3. Place a copy of page 42 face up on each child's desk. Ask children to put a check next to the animals they think have a backbone.

4. Give each child a copy of page 43. Have children stack the papers with page 42 on top, being careful to match the edges, and hold them up to a light. (A window works well.) Ask: *Which animals have backbones? Which ones don't? Can you remember the name for the animals you see that don't have a backbone?* (invertebrates)

TIP: To make mini peek-through animal pictures, have children cut out both cards (from page 42 and 43) for the animals that have backbones. Have them glue the front of each backbone card to the back of the matching animal card (placing glue on the edges only). When they hold up the cards to a window, what do they see? (*the animals' backbones*)

Literature Connection Solve the undersea mystery revealed in *Lobster's Secret* by Kathleen Hollenbeck (Soundprints, 1996). Invite children to predict what they think the lobster's secret will be. After reading, discuss the secret and why the lobster needed to keep it.

ACTIVITY Extension Explain that many invertebrates cannot move on their own to defend themselves or escape from predators. For this reason, some invertebrates have tentacles to sting intruders. Others have spiky bodies to make biting into them unpleasant and painful. Demonstrate defense and protection by making a sea urchin from toothpicks and clay. Give each child a 3-inch ball of clay and 15 toothpicks. Have children roll the clay into a ball to make the body of a sea urchin. Ask children to insert toothpicks on all sides of the sea urchin's body. Let them tell how they think these "spines" help sea urchins protect themselves from predators.

Make Your Own Jellyfish

Pour gelatin into a sandwich bag for a hands-on encounter with a colorful jellyfish!

Materials

◎ gelatin

◎ water

◎ glass bowl

◎ spoon

◎ resealable sandwich bags

Teaching the Lesson

1 Ask children to place a hand behind their back and feel their backbone. Ask: *Is your backbone hard or soft? What do you think your backbone helps you to do?* Discuss the idea that human backbones support the body, holding it upright.

2 Invite children to think about invertebrates, animals without backbones. Ask: *Would you expect an invertebrate to feel hard or soft if you touched it? Why do you say that?*

3 Two hours before the lesson, make several batches of gelatin. For each batch, use a large box of gelatin. Mix it as follows: Dissolve gelatin in ¼ cup water. Place it in a microwave and cook on high for 30 seconds. Stir well. Add 1¼ cups cold water, and stir again. Pour into several resealable sandwich bags. Chill until cold and partially jelled.

4 Hand out the bags and let children pass them around the room without opening them. Explain that these feel similar to the body of a jellyfish. Reinforce vocabulary by again asking children what this kind of animal is called. (*invertebrate*) It does not have a backbone, and it floats on the sea.

Learning Center Link

Ocean Life

Reinforce science vocabulary and spelling skills with a word-building game. Write the word invertebrate on jellyfish-shaped pieces of paper, one letter per piece. Place the letters in an envelope labeled "Invertebrate." Let children visit in pairs or independently to build words with the letters. Have them record words they make. Remind them to make the big word, too!

Literature Connection

Read aloud Twig C. George's *Jellies: The Story of Jellyfish* (Millbrook Press, 2000). Then invite children to stand up and sway to soft music, imitating the up and down motion of jellyfish floating with the currents. Eventually change the music, and have children move as other creatures of the sea.

ACTIVITY Extension

Provide paper plates and colored streamers. Let children tape 12-inch streamers around the plates, representing jellyfish and their tentacles. Explain that tentacles help protect jellyfish. Lined with stinging cells that sting whatever they touch, tentacles injure or scare away predators and people. Let children put the jellyfish on their heads and walk around the classroom, observing how tentacles (streamers) brush against people as they walk by.

SCIENCE NOTES

Invertebrates can be tough to figure out. *Where are their mouths? How do they eat?* Share these facts with students to help answer their questions.

- A clam extends long tubes from its shell to take in water and tiny bits of sea life.

- The mouth of a jellyfish is underneath its body. As the jellyfish floats, it eats food that it comes into contact with. Tentacles also bring food to its mouth.

- An octopus catches food with its tentacles.

- The oyster's shell is partly open so the oyster can draw water inside. Sticky hairs on its gills catch tiny bits of plankton.

- The crab uses pincers on its front legs to grab its prey. It passes the food back to the mouth, which is under the animal's body.

Oyster Math

Use these "oysters" with multiple "pearls" to reinforce the concept of odd and even.

Materials

- Oyster Math reproducible (see page 44)
- white plastic beads
- 3-ounce paper cups
- glue
- crayons

Learning Center Link

Bring in a variety of abandoned (and clean) sea animal shells, such as those of a hermit crab, mussel, clam, snail, oyster, barnacle, shrimp, and scallop. Glue each to a small square of cardboard and place carefully in a shoebox in the Learning Center. During free time, encourage children to work alone or in pairs to study the shells and arrange or sort them by size, color, shape, and texture. They can turn this activity into a game by taking turns sorting the shells and letting their partners guess the sorting rule. Make writing tools and paper available for those who feel inspired to write a poem or story about a shell's former inhabitant.

Teaching the Lesson

1. Give each child a copy of the reproducible and a cupful of beads.

2. Have children glue beads onto each oyster to match the numeral below it.

3. Ask children to draw lines between each pair of pearls in the oyster.

4. If every pearl has a partner, the number of pearls in the oyster is even. Children should write the word *even* on the line. If an oyster has a pearl without a partner, the numeral is odd. Children should write the word *odd* on the line.

ACTIVITY Extension

Use the "pearls" for more math practice. Give children additional beads and shell-shaped cutouts. Share word problems for children to solve—for example, *I found 5 pearls in one oyster and 7 in another. How many more pearls did I find in the second oyster? How many did I find all together?* Have children use the beads and shell shapes to show the math. After you share a couple of word problems, let children take turns sharing more.

Wind and Waves

Generate wind and watch its effect on water.

Materials

◎ 9- by 13-inch rectangular glass pan

◎ water

◎ food coloring

Teaching the Lesson

1 Fill the pan half full with water. Place it on a table where everyone can see it. Let a volunteer put several drops of food coloring into the water. DO NOT STIR.

2 Immediately ask one child to blow on the water in an attempt to make it move. Add more children to the task until the water ripples and the color begins to move.

3 Invite children to observe what takes place. Ask: *How does the water change when we blow on it? What happens to the food coloring? Why do you think it is moving?*

4 Help children associate this activity with the effect of wind on the sea and the way it propels jellyfish and other floating sea creatures.

Literature Connection Take children on a tour of jellyfish around the world with *Jellies: The Story of Jellyfish* by Twig C. George (The Millbrook Press, 2000). Read the book aloud and allow children time to study the photographs and discuss what they see. Interview them on tape as they pretend they are jellyfish: *How does it feel to float in the sea? What do you see as you float? Where do you go? What do you eat? Who tries to eat you?*

TIP: Wrap up this section of your theme unit by singing the fourth verse of the theme song. Practice the first three, too! (See page 11.)

Song of the Sea
(to the tune of "B-I-N-G-O")

Invertebrates are soft inside
Because they have no backbone.
Starfish, octopus,
Lobster, crab, and clam,
They crawl, float, and swim.
Invertebrates they all are.

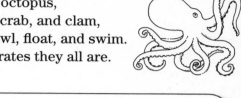

 **Learning Center Link**

Children turn a handprint into a fanciful octopus with paint and a little imagination.

◎ *Set up the center by filling several pie plates with an inch or so of paint in various colors.*

◎ *Add construction or painting paper and paintbrushes.*

◎ *Demonstrate the activity by dipping your hand (held flat) in the paint and pressing it on a sheet of paper. Turn the paper around (so the top is now the bottom) to see the body of an octopus. When the paint is dry, dip a thumb in a different color paint and press it on the octopus to make two eyes. Dip pinkies in paint to make the iris of each eye. Use a paintbrush to add sea scenery.*

◎ *Have children try the activity on their own. Labeling elements of the picture will provide practice in using science vocabulary. (Write words such as octopus and seaweed on chart paper and post for reference.)*

◎ *Children can go further by writing (or dictating) stories to go with their pictures.*

Name_____ Date_____

No Bones About It!

shark

crab

octopus

flounder

seahorse

barracuda

Early Themes: Ocean Life Scholastic Professional Books

No Bones About It!

Oyster Math

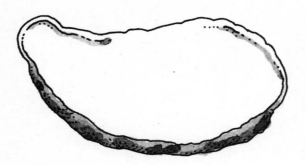

6 _____

1 _____

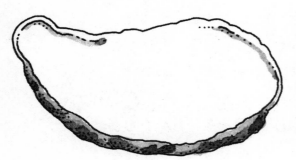

3 _____

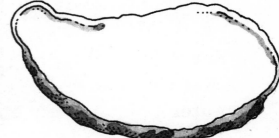

4 _____

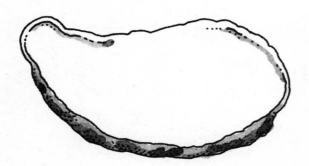

5 _____

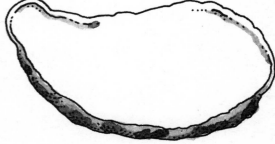

2 _____

Early Themes: Ocean Life Scholastic Professional Books

Ocean Life Celebration

Wrap up your unit on ocean life with a day of fun and exciting activities revolving around life at sea. Set the tone with games, decorations, and music. Solve the riddles on the poster (bound in center), play sea life card games, share sea stories, and more. Invite visitors in to see children's artwork and ocean projects. Wrap up with a rousing chorus of "Song of the Sea." (See page 11.)

Throughout your Ocean Life Celebration, set the scene with thematic background music such as "Sea and Dolphins" (part of the *Sounds of the Earth* series; Oreade Music, 1999).

Teaching With the Poster:
What Do You See in the Sea?

Use the poster (bound in center) to explore the sea, then let children create their own informative posters to learn more.

Teaching the Lesson

1. Share background information to help students learn more about the deep sea and enhance their enjoyment of the poster. (See Science Notes, right.)

2. Invite children to identify animals they know. What animals are new to them? Challenge children to solve the riddles, taking turns pointing out the sea creatures that match each description:

◎ A fish with eight arms: cirrate octopod

◎ Six fish that glow: deep sea anglerfish, gulper eel, lanternfish, deep sea jellyfish, deep sea hatchetfish, bristlemouth

◎ Three whales: sperm whale, blue whale, Dall's porpoise

◎ Animals that look like plants: pom-pom anemone, sea cucumber

3. Invite children to work together to write new riddles for classmates to solve. The riddles need not be elaborate or rhyming—for example, "This animal looks like a vegetable," would suffice for a sea cucumber. Let children add their riddles to the poster display.

SCIENCE NOTES

Only the hardiest of creatures can live in the deep sea. Dolphins leap near the surface and dive deep for food; tiny fish and sponges near the ocean floor barely move—subdued by the bitter cold and the pressure of so much water above them. At the greatest depths, there is total darkness. Here anglerfish, lanternfish, jellyfish, and some shrimp emit their own heatless light.

ACTIVITY Extension Let children revisit what they've learned, and take a special area of interest further, by creating their own posters. Divide the class into groups, and ask children in each group to work together to create a poster that represents life in a specific layer of the sea. For example, children exploring the shore might show the high tide zone, which extends up on the rocks and sand. Animals that live here include sand crabs, polychaete worms, sand dollars, moon snails, pismo clams, gulls, and beach hoppers (which look like mini-shrimp). Children exploring the kelp forest can show sea otters, red abalone, blue rockfish, and the gumboot chiton (the largest chiton in the world). Children exploring the open sea can include plankton, leatherback sea turtle, purple-striped jelly, Pacific white-sided dolphin, blue shark, and so on.

Learning Center Link

Cut 3- by 5-inch index cards in half, and provide 12 halves for each child. Ask children to choose six sea animals from the poster and draw each animal on two separate cards to make six matching pairs. (If possible, have children write one fact about the animal on each card as well.) Working independently, have children mix up their 12 cards, place them facedown on the desk, and lift them to find the matching animals. Divide the class into small groups and let children combine and shuffle their cards to play the same memory game or the card game "Go Fish."

ART

Fish Frolic

Decorate a tablecloth with sea life and serve foods with a seaside theme.

Materials

- ◎ white paper tablecloth
- ◎ tempera paint
- ◎ fine markers
- ◎ thematic snack foods (fish-shaped crackers, mozzarella cheese, pretzels, blue punch)

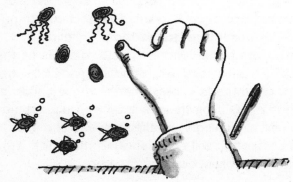

Teaching the Lesson

1. Several days before the event, send home a note inviting each family to sign up to bring a theme-related snack—such as fish-shaped crackers, sea urchins made by pressing pretzel sticks into squares of mozzarella cheese, blue-colored beverages, sugar cookies cut in a starfish shape, and cut-up fruit served on a fish-shaped platter.

2. Spread the tablecloth on a long table in your classroom.

3. Provide paint in several colors. Have children press their thumbs into the paint and onto the tablecloth to make dozens of thumbprints in a variety of colors.

4. Let children use fine-point markers to add features to their thumbprints, turning them into jellyfish, octopus, sharks, and other sea animals.

5. When the tablecloth dries, set the table for a seaside feast!

CREATIVE MOVEMENT

Fishy, Fishy!

Involve your entire class in fun and frolic with two popular and easy-to-play action games.

Teaching the Lesson

1. Play "Fishy, Fishy, in the Sea." Prepare the game area by drawing two horizontal lines of chalk on the playground or floor. The lines should be far apart from each other. Have the entire class stand on one line. Choose three children to be "sharks" while the rest are "fish." Have sharks stand halfway between the lines, facing the fish. To start the game, the sharks call, "Fishy, fishy, in the sea. I'll bet you can't get past me!" At once, the

fish begin to run, trying to get to the other side before they are tagged by a shark. Those tagged take the place of the sharks, and the game begins again.

2 Play "Prey, Prey, Predator!" This game follows the format of the traditional "Duck, Duck, Goose!" Before each round of play, invite the group to select a different predator and its prey. These will be the names the tagger says while walking around the circle, tapping heads. Instead of "Duck, duck, goose!" the tagger might say, "Clam, clam, otter!"

Literature Connection Just the facts, and bold, bright illustrations, are what you'll find in *Sharks* by Gail Gibbons (Holiday House, 1993). Beginning readers will gain information about sharks from both pictures and text, simply written and geared for the young learner.

LANGUAGE ARTS

I'm Going to the Ocean

Play a simple game of ABC order, with an ocean theme.

Teaching the Lesson

1 Have children sit in a circle. Start the game with the sentence, "I'm going to the ocean, and I think I'll see an albatross." Write the word *albatross* on chart paper, and underline the first letter, *a*.

2 Going clockwise around the circle, have each child repeat the original phrase and add a sea animal that begins with the next letter of the alphabet. Continue from A to Z, helping as needed, and writing each addition on the chart.

TIP: Sample sea animals from A to Z follow.

A: albatross, anemone
B: blue whale, barnacle
C: cormorant, clam
D: dolphin, dragonfish
E: eel
F: flounder, flying fish
G: grouper, goby
H: hammerhead shark, herring
I: iguana, icefish
J: jellyfish
K: krill
L: lobster, limpet
M: manatee, mussel
N: narwhal
O: octopus, otter
P: penguin, plankton
Q: quahog, queen angelfish
R: ray, reptile
S: shark, starfish
T: turtle, tuna
U: urchin
V: viper fish
W: whale, walrus
X: (Children might invent a fish name for this letter.)
Y: yellowfin tuna
Z: zooplankton

Literature Connection Fans of "find the hidden picture" books will delight in *Find Demi's Sea Creatures* by Demi (Putnam & Grosset, 1991), a collection of sea creature games that challenge readers to find more than 20 animals of the sea, from swordfish to manatees. Place the book in the Learning Center where children can enjoy it on their own or with a classmate. Families joining your class for the sea life celebration will enjoy sharing the book with their children.

You are a beautiful blessing
to the world!

Rebecca White Ahn

Child of Mine, Know This

Rebecca Gittrich Whitecotton

Bright Treasures

Child of Mine, Know This

ISBN-10: 0-9725450-1-8
ISBN-13: 978-0-9725450-1-3
Library of Congress Control Number: 2005909349

Photographs (numbered in order of appearance, starting with cover) courtesy of and copyright ©
Rebecca Whitecotton (15-17, 28, 34-36, 55), Carrie Punches (2, 51), Marcie Gittrich (19, 20, 39),
Lori Damigo (26), Robin C. Ocepek (48), Shutterstock (1, 3-6, 9-14, 18, 21, 23, 25, 27, 29, 31-33,
37, 38, 40, 41, 43-47, 49, 50, 52-54, 56), Big Stock Photo (7, 8, 22, 24, 30, 42).

With thanks to Randy Whitecotton for support, patience and an open mind. — rgw

Printed in China through Global Ink, Inc. USA

Bright Treasures
P.O. Box 2445 • Palatine, Illinois 60078
publisher@brighttreasures.net

www.brighttreasures.net   www.childofmineknowthis.net

To Ethan and Alison, my children of light —

may I always remember my promises to you.

— rgw

Child of mine, know this —

You are not a child
 in the eyes of the universe,
 in the arms of God,
 in the heart of All That Is.

You are a brilliant light that has been
shining since the beginning of time.

You are a wise
and ancient soul
who has come
to this earth yet
another time to
shine your light on
all humanity.

The body you have chosen for this life now looks like a child,
for that is how the cycle of human life begins.
Though our bodies look different now,
we are no different inside.

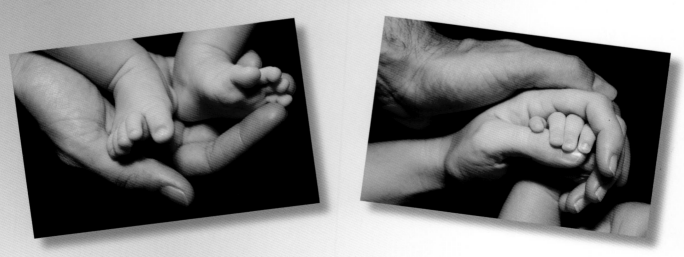

We are both the light of God, the soul of the universe,
expressing ourselves on earth.

Through my human eyes I see you as a child.

Through my spiritual eyes
– the eyes of God –
I see you as an ageless expression of love.

Child of mine, know this —

You chose your life.
You chose this family.
You chose to be with me.

Your choice is a beautiful blessing.

I, too, chose my life.
I chose my family.
I chose to be with you.

Through thousands of years we have taken on different roles on earth, sometimes together, sometimes apart.

In other lifetimes
you may have been
my parent, and I
may have been your
child. We may have
been brothers,
sisters, enemies
or friends.

I am connected to
you eternally.

Child of mine, know this —

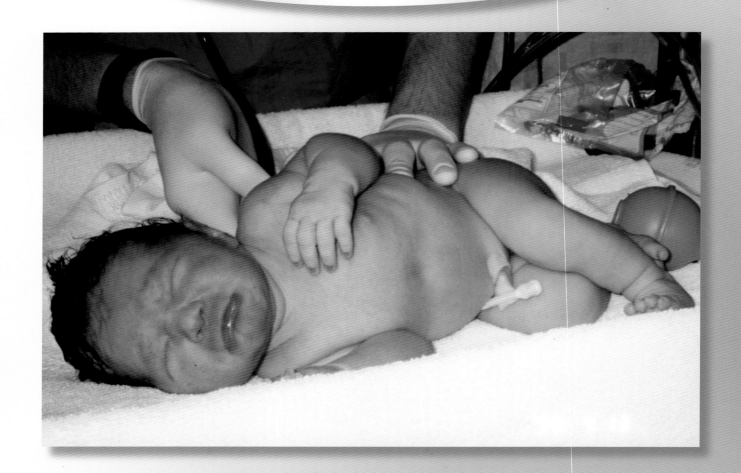

When we are born into our human bodies
it is easy to forget.
We forget where we came from.
We forget who we really are.
We forget that we chose this life, this situation, this family.
We forget why we came, and what we are to do.

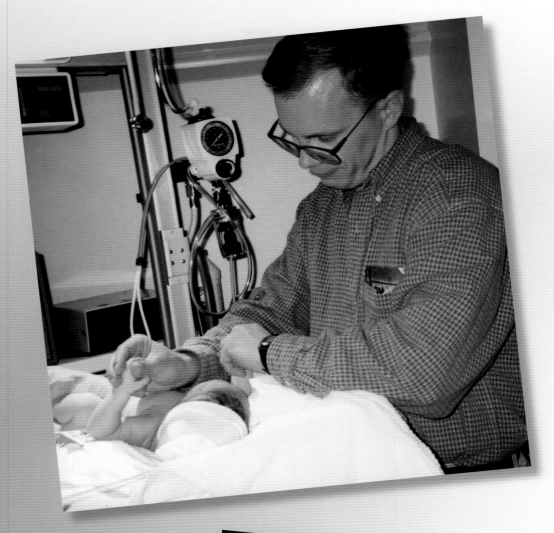

We are here
to remind
each other
who we
really are.

I am here to
remind you
of your
greatness,
of your
connection to
All That Is.

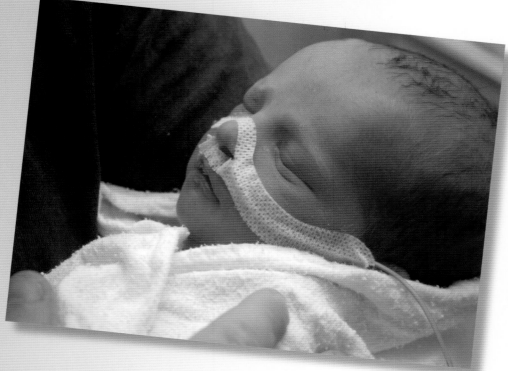

You are here to
remind me that my
spirit is bigger
and more powerful
than my physical
body.

We are here, together, to walk through this illusion
in search of a grander reality.

Child of mine, know this —

Before this lifetime began,
I made you a promise.

I promised
to be the best parent
that I could be.

I promised to teach you
the ways of the
world as I know it.

I promised to help you build a strong character
and discover your talents and abilities.

I promised to keep your body safe and out of danger.

I promised to challenge you and make you think deeply.

I promised to help you find the experiences
that will allow you to do what you came to do in this lifetime.

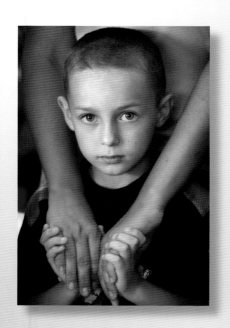

I promised to do all these things,
knowing that many times you would be angry with me
for treating you like a child.

I made these promises knowing that many times I would forget what I promised and make choices that don't honor the true spirit in each of us.

Before this lifetime began, you made me a promise.

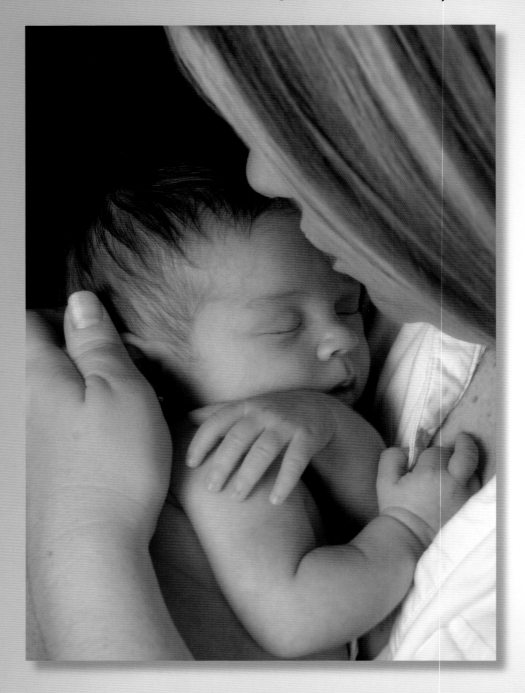

You promised to remind me of where I came from
with your childlike innocence.

You promised to show me the meaning of
unconditional love by allowing me to love you.

You promised to challenge my assumptions about the world and make me think deeply about who I am.

You promised to help me find the experiences that will allow me to do what I came to do in this lifetime.

You promised to do all these things,
knowing that many times I would be angry with you
for acting like a child, and for challenging
the illusions that I have come to believe are real.

You made these promises knowing that many times
you would forget what you promised
and make choices that don't honor the true spirit in each of us.

child of mine, know this —

We can keep our promises if we remember who we are.

We can keep our promises if we look at each
other through the eyes of God.

I am
no better than you,
no older than you,
no wiser than you.

We are but individual
expressions of the
same substance
that fills the entire
universe.

We are not separate.
We are one.

You are not a child
in the eyes of the universe,
in the arms of God,
in the heart of All That Is.

I look at you
with love.

I know
who you are.

You are a beautiful blessing
to the world.